DIFFICULT &
DANGEROUS

# DESPERATE
## ESCAPES

### SIMON LEWIS

A+

**Smart Apple Media**

Smart Apple Media is published by Black Rabbit Books
P.O. Box 3263, Mankato, Minnesota 56002

Printed in Hong Kong

Library of Congress Cataloging-in-Publication Data

Lewis, Simon.
    Desperate escapes / Simon Lewis.
    p. cm.—(Smart Apple Media. Difficult & dangerous)
    Includes index.
    ISBN 978-1-59920-158-0
    1.  Escapes—Case studies—Juvenile literature.  I. Title.
HV8657. L54 2009
365'.641—dc22

                                                                            2008000432

Created by Q2AMedia
Series Editor: Jean Coppendale
Book Editor: Corrine Ochiltree
Senior Art Designers: Ashita Murgai, Nishant Mudgal
Designer: Shilpi Sarkar
Picture Researcher: Lalit Dalal
Line Artists: Amit Tayal, Sibi N.D
Illustrators: Mahender Kumar, Sanyogita Lal

All words in **bold** can be found in the glossary on pages 30–31.

Picture credits
t=top b=bottom c=center l=left r=right m=middle
Cover: Q2A Media
Visual&Written SL/ Alamy: 4, Hulton Archive/ Stringer/ Getty Images: 5t, Maureen Photography: 5b,
Danita Delimont/ Alamy: 8t, 8b, Photos 12/ Alamy: 10t, Danita Delimont/ Alamy: 10b, RAF Museum: 11b,
Associated Press: 16, 17t, 18, Bettmann/ Corbis: 19, Kapoor Baldev/ Sygma/ Corbis: 20t, Pavel K/ Shutterstock: 20b,
Bettmann/ Corbis: 21t, 21b, 24t, Tomasz Szymanski/ Shutterstock: 24b, Mick Barnard/ Nordicphotos: 25,
Roger Hutchings/ Alamy: 26, AFP/ Getty Images: 27t, National Geographic/ Getty Images: 27b, AFP/
Getty Images: 28

9 8 7 6 5 4 3 2 1

# Contents

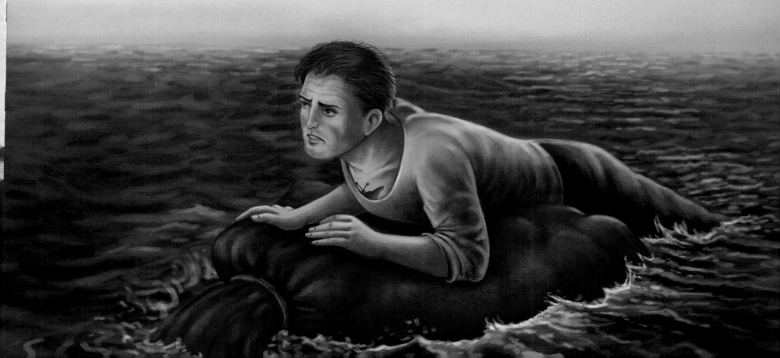

# BID FOR FREEDOM

*Throughout history, prisoners of all kinds have made plans to escape from every type of prison. Some plans have been simple, some have been difficult, and many have been extremely dangerous.*

## Daring Escapes

Henri Charriere, known as Papillon, was a criminal imprisoned for a murder he denied committing. The Anglin brothers and Frank Morris were vicious criminals imprisoned in **Alcatraz** for violent robberies. All spent most of their lives in prison thinking of ways to escape. They were sent to prisons that were thought to be escape proof, but by cunning and careful planning they all managed spectacular escapes that left the authorities reeling.

*These cells are typical of those found inside Alcatraz prison. Frank Morris and brothers John and Clarence Anglin would have served their sentences in cells like these, while hatching their plan to escape.*

4

# Prisoners of War

Not all prisoners are criminals. They may be soldiers or innocent **civilians** caught up in the horrors of war. Captured by the enemy, they may spend many years in prison until they either escape or the war ends. The prisoners in **Stalag Luft** III, a World War II prisoner-of-war camp, and Dith Pran, a political prisoner in Cambodia, used bravery and determination to survive and overcome even the most brutal captors.

*Stalag Luft III prisoner-of-war camp in Germany. It was run by the **Luftwaffe** for captured **Allied** airmen until April 29, 1945.*

## Forced to Flee

For some, escaping means leaving a home they love to go to a safe place. The **Dalai Lama** was forced to flee Tibet when the Chinese invaded his country. He escaped through the Himalaya Mountains to India, where he lives today. Since his escape, the Dalai Lama has shared his experiences to highlight the troubles in Tibet.

# KING OF ESCAPES

Henri Charriere (1906–73) was born in the south of France. He joined the French navy at age 17, but hated navy life. He left as soon as he could. Henri then drifted into a life of crime and became known as Papillon (French for butterfly) because of a butterfly tattoo on his chest.

Papillon first went to prison when he was 24. For the next 13 years, he lived in some of the most brutal prisons in the world.

## The First Escape

At age 24, Papillon was accused of murder, a crime he denied, and sentenced to a life of **hard labor**. He was sent to a **penal colony** in French Guiana. Together with two other prisoners, he escaped in a boat along the Cayenne River to the Atlantic Ocean, where they headed for Colombia. On their journey they were helped by a group of **lepers**. As they left, Papillon shook a leper's hand. In those days, this was thought to be a dangerous act that could have given him the dreadful disease.

## Imprisoned Again

They were recaptured and sent to another, tougher, prison in Colombia. Here, in one of several failed escape attempts, Papillon reached the top of the prison wall when guards began to shoot at him. He jumped to avoid the bullets and broke both his feet.

### Escape Route

When Papillon escaped from French Guiana, he sailed along the coast via Trinidad. From there, he reached Colombia, where he was recaptured before escaping again. He lived happily in the Guajira region of northern Colombia with a tribe of Indians for several months before he was recaptured.

*French Guiana, in South America, has a hot, humid climate. Prisoners in the penal colony had to work in sweltering heat.*

7

# Solitary Confinement

As a punishment for his escape attempts, Papillon was sentenced to two years in **solitary confinement**. In this small, hot, dark cell, with thick stone walls, he slept on a plank of wood and had only a cement block to sit on and a **chamber pot**. Rations were soup and stale bread. Huge centipedes crawled over the prisoners as they slept. Prisoners often went mad or nearly starved to death.

The thick stone walls of the solitary confinement cells meant prisoners stayed in complete silence. Many went mad.

## Rescue from Sharks

Papillon survived, only to be sentenced to solitary confinement again for killing a prisoner. He was given eight years, which he could never survive. After 18 months, the inmates were allowed to swim in the sea for an hour a day, in an area protected from sharks. During one swim, Papillon raced to the rescue of a girl who fell into the shark-infested sea just beyond. As a reward, he was released from solitary but was sent to a prison on Devil's Island. No one had ever escaped from this island, which was edged by high cliffs and jagged rocks.

Devil's Island, off the coast of French Guiana, was the last place where dangerous criminals were sent. Its rocky coastline prevented most prisoners from escaping.

## Escape from Devil's Island

Papillon believed he could escape from anywhere. After spending many months watching the sea, he had a brilliant idea. The island had an **inlet** where waves rushed in and out. He noticed that the seventh wave was always much higher than the others, high enough to carry a person over the rocks and out to sea. He built a raft from coconut shells. One night as a 39-foot (12-m) high wave crashed down before him, he threw his raft and himself on top of the swell. Papillon clung to his flimsy raft and was carried out to sea. He spent nearly 60 hours afloat after leaving Devil's Island and was badly burnt by the sun. Eventually, Papillon reached the safety of the mainland of French Guiana.

*Papillon built a raft made from empty coconut shells, which he stuffed into a large sack. The raft was just large enough for his body to float on.*

*"My lips were already cracking and this was still the cool of the night. My lips and eyes burned painfully. It was the same with my hands and forearms . . ."*

From his biography, *Papillon* (1970), describing his time on the raft after escaping from Devil's Island.

# Freedom at Last

Once on land, Papillon traveled west to Venezuela. Before long, he was captured and put in prison again. But fate was about to take a hand. A new Venezuelan government decided to free Papillon on the condition that he lived in a village for a year to make sure that he behaved. Once he had proved himself, Papillon had the freedom to travel anywhere in Venezuela. Finally, at the age of 37, the butterfly was free. Papillon wrote a best-selling book about his time in prison, which was made into a very successful film.

When he was a free man, Papillon married and had a daughter. He died in 1973, at age 67.

## How Would YOU Cope?

Papillon survived his time in solitary confinement by keeping to a strict daily routine. This included walking to keep fit and remembering his past life to stop himself from going mad.

1. How would you survive in solitary confinement? Plan a typical day.

2. What do you think you would find most difficult?
   - not being able to talk
   - not going outside
   - missing your friends and family
   - the horrible food
   - being confined in a small space

# ESCAPE FROM STALAG III

*Roger Bushell (1910–44) was born in South Africa. He was educated in Johannesburg and later studied law at Cambridge University. Bushell was an outstanding fighter pilot. But he would go down in history as the leader of one of the most famous war escapes ever.*

## War Is Declared

World War II began in 1939. On May 23, 1942, Flight Lieutenant Roger Bushell was ordered to patrol the French coastline with his squadron of 12 **Spitfire** planes. None of the airmen had ever flown in **combat** before. German planes soon attacked them. After several long air battles, Bushell's plane was badly damaged and started to spiral out of control. He managed to land the plane safely, but he was inside enemy territory. A German patrol saw him land, and he was dragged from his plane and sent to an **interrogation center** in Germany.

### Emergency Landing

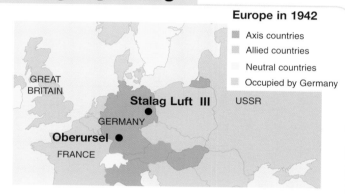

**Europe in 1942**
- Axis countries
- Allied countries
- Neutral countries
- Occupied by Germany

GREAT BRITAIN

Stalag Luft III

GERMANY

USSR

Oberursel ●

FRANCE

Most captured Allied airmen were taken straight to **Dulag Luft** interrogation center at Oberursel in Germany (the main **Axis** country). The men were stripped and questioned. Some of the men were kept in solitary confinement. Others were then taken to Stalag Luft camps.

*Roger Bushell with his Spitfire. He was the commanding officer of 92 Squadron when he was shot down in 1940.*

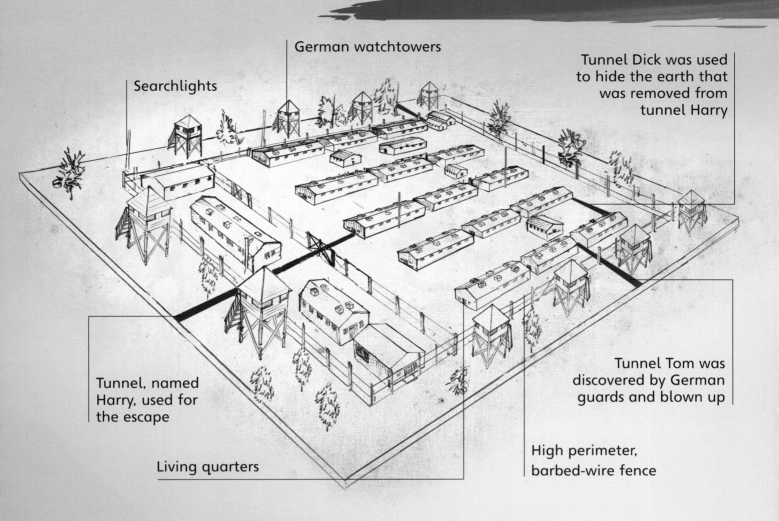

Searchlights

German watchtowers

Tunnel Dick was used to hide the earth that was removed from tunnel Harry

Tunnel, named Harry, used for the escape

Living quarters

Tunnel Tom was discovered by German guards and blown up

High perimeter, barbed-wire fence

A sketch of a model of the Stalag Luft III prisoner-of-war camp. The main tunnel was dug in a straight line from the living quarters to just outside the camp.

## Muddy Tunnel

When Bushell arrived at Dulag Luft, an escape committee was already working on a tunnel. Digging the tunnel was dirty, dark, hot, and dangerous work. The tunnel frequently flooded and was eventually abandoned. Bushell made two more unsuccessful escape attempts before he was sent to Stalag Luft III, where he put into action everything that he had learned about tunneling techniques and escape plans.

Stalag Luft III held captured Allied air force men. It was built in the middle of a huge pine forest, 100 miles (160 km) southeast of Berlin.

*"Everyone here is living on borrowed time. By rights we should all be dead!"*
Roger Bushell at the first meeting of the Escape Committee

## The Master Plan

Working with a group of other prisoners, Bushell decided to build three long, deep tunnels all at the same time. The idea was that if one tunnel was discovered, they could continue with the other two. The guards would not think that two tunnels were being dug at the same time—and certainly not three! Bushell's plan was that more than 200 men would escape, all with civilian clothes and **forged papers** so they could get out of Germany.

## Tom, Dick, and Harry

The tunnels were code-named Tom, Dick, and Harry, and the prisoners began work on them in 1943. To speed up the escape, they worked mainly on Tom. This tunnel had reached the edge of the camp when microphones, placed there to pick up underground noises, alerted the guards that something was going on. The German guards swooped in, discovered the entrance to the tunnel, and then blew it up with explosives.

A light system was eventually rigged up, but at the beginning, candles were used for light.

*Tin cans, spoons, and other everyday objects were used for digging.*

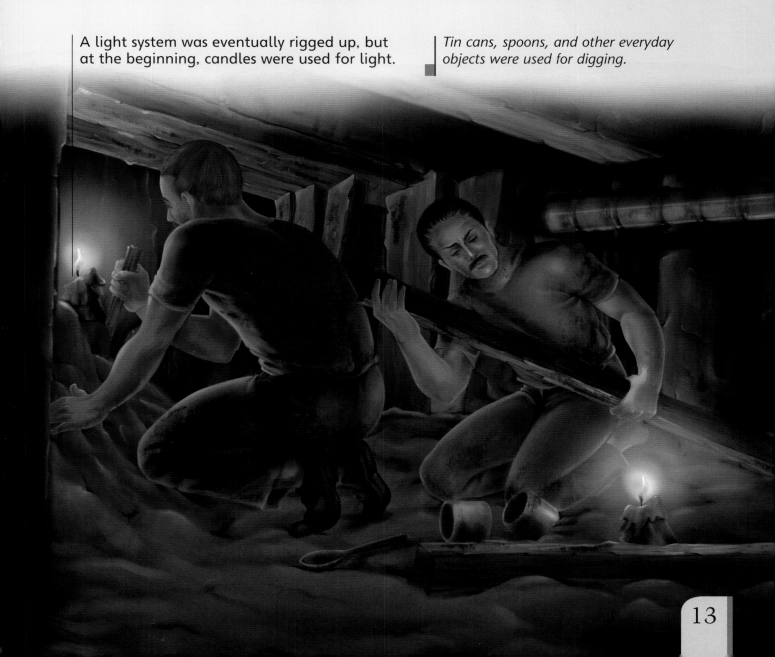

# Under Suspicion

Work continued on Harry, but the guards suspected something was going on. They moved 20 men who they thought were the **ringleaders** to different living quarters. But, in fact, only four of them were key workers. While the tunnel was being dug, other prisoners were making civilian clothes, creating maps, forging papers, making compasses, and preparing forged money. On March 24, 1944, Harry was ready.

## Stay or Go?

Bushell had to decide if they should attempt the escape or not. The weather was cold and the ground was covered in thick snow. If they left, then they would leave footprints. If they did not, they would have to wait until the next new moon, by which time the tunnel might have been found or might have collapsed. Bushell decided to go. The date, Friday, March 24, 1944, was stamped on the forged papers and more than 200 prisoners prepared to escape.

# A Tragic End

Bushell escaped from Stalag Luft with a French air force pilot, both disguised as French businessmen. Once through the tunnel, they headed for the woods and then to the city of Saarbrücken by train. Meanwhile, 76 other men escaped through the tunnel before the German guards discovered it. Unfortunately, nearly all of the prisoners were recaptured—only three reached safety. Fifty escapees, including Bushell, were shot following orders given directly by Adolf Hitler, although this was against all the rules of war.

*Some of the prisoners were captured as they scrambled out of the tunnel.*

## Could YOU Escape?

Imagine you are planning a big escape from your classroom and that your teacher is the guard.
Draw a plan of the school.

- How would you get past the guard?
- Where would your tunnel go?
- Once outside the classroom, what would you do?
- If you had to wear a disguise, what would you choose?

# FLIGHT FROM TIBET

*Tibet is a small, peaceful country deep in the heart of the Himalaya mountains. Its leader is the Dalai Lama. In 1950, the Chinese People's Liberation Army (CPLA) marched into Tibet and took it over by force, claiming it belonged to China. More than 2,000 people were killed in the first three days of fighting.*

## Dangerous Times

**Buddhist** temples were destroyed, villages overturned, and the Dalai Lama taken prisoner. Rumors quickly spread that the Dalai Lama would be taken to China where he would be kept as a prisoner and maybe even killed. He had to escape from Tibet for his own safety.

## Escape into Night

At 10 P.M. on March 17, 1959, the Dalai Lama left Norbulingka Palace in Lhasa where he had been held by the Chinese as a prisoner. He disguised himself as a soldier, swapping his monk's robes for trousers and a dark overcoat. He slung a rifle over his shoulder and took off his glasses. Joined by several cabinet ministers and people to protect him, the Dalai Lama was smuggled out of the palace. He reached the outskirts of the city where his family was waiting with ponies for their long and dangerous journey.

*The Dalai Lama (b. 1936) is a Buddhist monk. Buddhism was the main religion in Tibet. Many believed he had been killed by the Chinese army before his escape.*

16

Thousands of Tibetan women silently surrounded the Potala Palace, the main residence of the Dalai Lama, to protest against Chinese invasion and repression on March 17, 1959 in Lhasa, Tibet. The Dalai Lama feared the Chinese forces would attack the people at the palace, so he decided to leave Tibet.

" . . . the odds against making a successful break seemed terrifyingly high. Then, slipping my glasses into my pocket, I stepped outside. I was very frightened. I was joined by two soldiers [his own] who silently escorted me to the gate . . . I groped my way across the park, hardly able to see a thing."

From the Dalai Lama's autobiography, *Freedom in Exile* (1990)

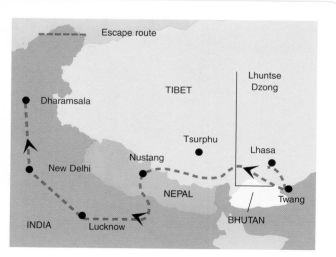

This map shows the Dalai Lama's escape route from Lhasa, in Tibet, to India.

# Into the Mountains

The Dalai Lama and his group had to journey through the treacherous Himalaya Mountains to India. After three days, they reached the Sabo-La Pass, where a blizzard made the journey almost impossible. Eventually, they reached Lhuntse Dzong where the group hoped to stay, but they heard that Chinese troops were close by. They were forced to keep going without any rest.

The Dalai Lama on a dzomo

## Fever!

The weather grew worse with strong winds, driving snow, and freezing temperatures. When the blizzards finally stopped, the group suffered terrible **snow glare** that almost blinded them. The path was steep, rocky, and slippery. The Dalai Lama had been fighting off sickness for days, but now, frozen and physically exhausted, he developed a fever and became very ill. Any delay was dangerous because Chinese soldiers were nearby, so the Dalai Lama was put on the back of a **dzomo** and carried the rest of the way across the border to India at the Khenzimana Pass.

*The Dalai Lama and his supporters struggled through the mountains on their 15-day journey to India.*

The Dalai Lama (left) with Indian
Prime Minister Jawaharlal Nehru
(1889–1964). Nehru allowed the
Dalai Lama to settle in India. More
than 80,000 Tibetan **refugees**
followed the Dalai Lama to India.

# A Life of Exile

Once in India, the Dalai Lama was greeted
by the Prime Minister, Jawaharlal Nehru,
who faced a difficult decision. He did not
want to upset the Chinese government by
taking sides with the Dalai Lama, but he
also had a duty to protect the Dalai Lama
and his people. In Tibet, there were reports
that the Chinese soldiers were killing the
Tibetan people and destroying historic
buildings. Thousands of Tibetans were
fleeing their country to seek refuge in
India. Meanwhile, a new leader, chosen
by the Chinese government, replaced the
Dalai Lama in Tibet.

# The Aftermath

Eventually the Dalai Lama and some of his followers settled in **exile**, at a place in Pradesh, in northern India, called Dharamsala, also known as Little Lhasa. The Dalai Lama was awarded the **Nobel Peace Prize** in 1989 and is negotiating with the Chinese government to return to his homeland one day. The Chinese still control Tibet and have banned all of the Dalai Lama's writings and photographs. More than 650 Buddhist monasteries have been destroyed and thousands of people have been killed by Chinese soldiers or died of starvation and torture.

*The Dalai Lama greeting the public in his home of Dharamsala, India.*

" . . . the morale of the Tibetan people within Tibet remains very strong. I therefore do not doubt that the day of our return is drawing ever closer, though of course we cannot say it is definite."

From *Freedom in Exile*

## What Would YOU Need to Survive?

The Dalai Lama trekked 900 miles (1,450 km) in 15 days. Plan a 15-day journey from Tibet to India.

• What food, clothing, and camping equipment would you need to cope with the mountains and freezing blizzards?

• How far could you travel each day?

• How would you keep everyone's spirits up?

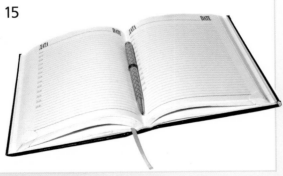

# ESCAPE FROM ALCATRAZ

*Dangerous criminals Frank Morris and brothers John and Clarence Anglin were sent to Alcatraz after attempting many other prison escapes. Alcatraz, a small island off the coast of San Francisco, was thought to be completely escape proof.*

Frank Morris (left), John Anglin (center), and Clarence Anglin (right) were all imprisoned for armed bank robbery.

## Spoons and Drills

Morris and the Anglin brothers were good at escaping. Between them, they hatched a brilliant plot to break out of Alcatraz. In 1960, they began to dig tunnels from the air vents in their cells that would lead them out into a little-used corridor. They used sharpened spoons for digging. One of them stole a motor from an old vacuum cleaner and made a drill to help them dig faster. They could only use the drill during the music hour so that the noise would not be heard. They also made dummy heads from toilet paper and soap to place on their own beds during the guards' prisoner count at night. The heads were painted using the prison art class paints and real hair was stuck on from bits collected from the floor of the barber's shop.

### Fooling the Guards

Two of the prisoners named their dummy heads "Oink" and "Oscar." These heads looked so realistic that the guards were fooled when they carried out their nightly head count of the prisoners.

# Rafts and Pumps

Once out of their cells, the escapees needed a way to get across the water. They built a raft from more than 50 raincoats belonging to the prisoners. Paddles were made from planks of wood. A stolen **concertina** was used to make a pump that would inflate the raft once they were outside the prison walls. On June 11, 1962, they were ready to go.

*Morris and the Anglin brothers planned to paddle from Alcatraz to the mainland, with a break on Angel Island.*

## Breakout!

After lights out, they put the dummy heads on their pillows and crawled along 30 feet (9 m) of plumbing through the vent tunnels up to the roof. They ran 98 feet (30 m) across the roof and then climbed down 49 feet (15 m) of piping, which brought them out near the shower area. This was the last time they were ever seen. The plan was to inflate the raincoat raft and paddle it to Angel Island. From here, they would head for Marin City through the Raccoon Straits. Once on the mainland, they would steal cars and some clothes and go their separate ways.

## Route to Freedom

This map shows the ambitious escape route planned by Frank Morris and Clarence and John Anglin. Both Angel Island and Alcatraz Island are in San Francisco Bay. Today, Angel Island is a National Park. Alcatraz Island has become a favorite sightseeing spot for tourists who are interested in discovering what life was like in Alcatraz.

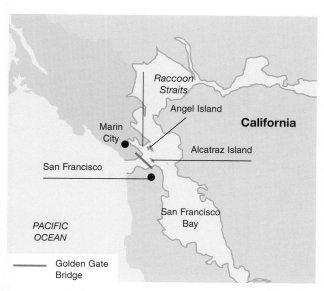

Raccoon Straits

Angel Island

**California**

Marin City

Alcatraz Island

San Francisco

San Francisco Bay

*PACIFIC OCEAN*

Golden Gate Bridge

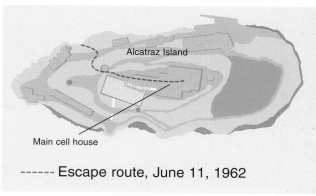

Alcatraz Island

Main cell house

------ Escape route, June 11, 1962

# The Search Is On!

As soon as the guards discovered the prisoners were missing, the **FBI** was informed and a full-scale search began. A paddle and a bag of personal letters were found between Alcatraz and Angel Island. No cars or clothes were stolen within 12 days of the escape, and the prisoners never contacted any friends or family. But no bodies were found either. Experts believe that swimmers could only survive in the freezing water for 20 minutes.

*A prison officer reveals the tiny hole in one of the cells used by the prisoners to escape.*

## The Rock

Alcatraz Island is also known as "the Rock." It is a small island 1.25 miles (2 km) from San Francisco, too far for an average person to swim. It became a prison for dangerous criminals in 1934. By the time it closed in 1963, it had held over 1,500 convicts. Only 14 escape attempts were ever made, and most of the escapees were shot by the guards or recaptured.

## Official Report

The official FBI report says that all three prisoners drowned while trying to escape. Some people believe that because no bodies have been found, there is a chance one or all of them made it to land.

## Floating Body

A Norwegian freighter reported seeing a body floating 20 miles (32 km) from the Golden Gate Bridge in July 1962. The body was floating face down in the water and was wearing denim trousers. This was the uniform that the prisoners at Alcatraz wore. No other person was reported missing or drowned at this time. The body was never recovered. Could this have been one of the escapees?

> "I believe . . . that these three men . . . made it off the island but never made it to shore. The tides and winds that night were strong, the convicts were not the athletic type. Only a trained athlete could make such a swim . . . The only swimming these fellows were accustomed to was little old creeks in the swamps of Florida and Louisiana."
>
> from Assistant Director Fred T. Wilkinson, Federal Bureau of Prisons, quoted in the press

### Could YOU Escape?

The escapees had to crawl through dark, narrow piping, run along a high roof at night, and cling to a raft in rough seas. If they suffered from any of the following fears and phobias, the escape would have been even harder to achieve.

Match the phobia to its correct meaning:

claustrophobia     fear of night

acrophobia     fear of darkness

noctiphobia     fear of water

aquaphobia     fear of narrow spaces

achluophobia     fear of heights

*Answers on page 32.*

# ROAD TO FREEDOM

*When a country is taken over by another, people can become prisoners in their own country. Dith Pran (b. 1942) was born in Angkor Wat in Cambodia, which was taken over by the fierce and ruthless Khmer Rouge army. The Khmer Rouge believed that the cities were breeding grounds for capitalism. They wanted all the people to live and work as peasants in the countryside.*

## Beginning of the End

On April 17, 1975, Khmer Rouge soldiers entered the city of Phnom Penh. The U.S. Embassy was **evacuated** and all foreign citizens were told to leave the country. Dith Pran worked as a translator and assistant to foreign journalists, including Sydney Schanberg, who was a reporter working for the *New York Times*. Schanberg helped to get Pran's family out of the country with him, but Dith Pran could not get a passport. Within days, the Khmer Rouge had taken control, government officials were executed, and everyone was forced to leave. Pran was sent to an unknown fate in the countryside.

*If the Khmer Rouge had found out that Dith Pran worked for foreign journalists, he would have been killed.*

*These people built canals in a labor camp in the countryside. Everyone, including children, the sick, and the elderly, was made to work.*

## The Khmer Rouge

This brutal **communist** group believed that everyone should be "peasants" who worked the land. They believed that people with an education, who could speak a foreign language, wore glasses, or worked in business were capitalists and enemies of communism. Money, religion, and **private enterprise** were all to be destroyed. Teachers, writers, and students were murdered. People were stripped of all their belongings. Their homes were destroyed and they were forced to march to villages to work. Any resistance was met with death. People were killed and buried in mass graves.

# Hunger and Murder

Dith Pran was now alone and a prisoner of the fierce and brutal Khmer Rouge. He pretended to the guards that he had been a taxi driver. He spoke little and did what he was told. After a month-long march, Pran stayed in a village called Dam Dek. In the villages, the Khmer Rouge organized groups who worked long hours doing hard labor with barely enough food and very little rest. People were beaten or killed for no reason. Many died of starvation every day. The Khmer Rouge soldiers forced people to marry—often just pairing up people by calling out names. Children were tricked into betraying their parents and were forced to become soldiers.

*"The villagers, desperate, ate snails, snakes, insects, rats, scorpions, tree bark, leaves, flower blossoms, the trunk of banana plants; sometimes they sucked the skin of a water buffalo. Reports reached Pran's village that to the west the famine was even more severe . . ."*

From *The Death and Life of Dith Pran* (1985), written by Sydney H. Schanberg

## A New Terror

In January 1979, the Vietnamese invaded Cambodia and overthrew the Khmer Rouge. Pran returned to his village to search for the rest of his extended family, but most had been killed or had died of starvation. The Vietnamese asked Pran to help them set up new systems in the villages to try to get the country back to normal. However, after about five months, they found out that Pran had worked with foreign journalists. He was forced to leave his job and, fearing for his life, he decided to escape to Thailand.

*The people of Phnom Penh celebrated when the Khmer Rouge forces entered the city on April 17, 1975. But their joy would soon turn to despair.*

## Escape to Freedom

One morning in September, Pran and 11 others began the dangerous journey to Thailand. They had to look out for Khmer Rouge **guerrillas**, Vietnamese soldiers, land mines, and **punji traps**. Finally, after 17 days, Pran crossed the border to Thailand. He could barely stand and was shaking with starvation. Dith Pran made it to the U.S., where he was reunited with his family. Sydney Schanberg wrote a story about the atrocities in Cambodia, which was made into a film, *The Killing Fields*.

*On the second day of their journey, a land mine exploded, killing two people and injuring Pran.*

## Could YOU Escape?

Could you survive a jungle escape? Answer a, b, or c.

What footwear would you take?
a) Rubber boots in case it rained
b) Slippers for warmth and comfort
c) Sturdy walking shoes

What food would you take?
a) Chocolate to keep your energy up
b) Instant ramen noodles
c) Dried fruit and nuts

What would be most useful?
a) A compass
b) A cell phone
c) A map

**Score**: *Mostly As*: Not bad, you stand a 50/50 chance of surviving.

*Mostly Bs*: Oh dear, best leave the escape plans to others.

*Mostly Cs*: Well done! You have the best chance of surviving.

# Glossary

**Alcatraz** a prison off the coast of San Francisco thought to be escape proof

**Allies** a group of countries, including the United States, that united against the Axis countries in World War II

**Axis** a group of countries that opposed the Allies, including Germany, Italy, and other European nations

**Buddhist** a person who believes in Buddhism, the religion that follows the teachings of Buddha

**capitalism** an economic system that is based on private businesses that make profits for themselves

**chamber pot** a container used for going to the toilet, usually used in bedrooms

**civilian** someone who does not belong to the army

**combat** a fight or a battle

**communists** supporters of communism, a system in which private ownership is not allowed

**concertina** a musical instrument similar to an accordian

**Dalai Lama** formerly the chief monk of Tibet who was overthrown by the Chinese People's Liberation Army

**Dulag Luft** an interrogation center in Germany where prisoners were taken when first captured

**dzomo** a strong animal that is a cross between a cow and a yak

**evacuate** to remove people from a place for reasons of safety

**exile** a punishment where someone is forced to live outside his or her own country

**FBI** Federal Bureau of Investigation, an American agency that looks after national security

**forged papers** false documents, such as passports or visas, designed to look like the real thing

**guerrillas** people who belong to unofficial armed groups that fight a regular army

**hard labor** very hard, physical work carried out by prisoners

**inlet** a strip of water leading from the sea into land

**interrogation center** a place where prisoners are questioned

**Khmer Rouge** a Cambodian communist group that overthrew the government in 1970

**leper** a person who suffers from the disease leprosy

**Luftwaffe** the German air force

**Nobel Peace Prize** a prize given to people from all over the world for their work in peace

**penal colony** a territory where prisoners were sent and made to work hard

**private enterprise** any privately owned business

**punji traps** sharpened bamboo sticks, covered in poison, hidden by bushes and leaves

**refugees** people who leave their own country and move to another for safety

**ringleaders** people who lead others in unlawful (or forbidden) activities

**snow glare** temporary blindness caused when bright sunlight is reflected by snow

**solitary confinement** a punishment in prisons, in which prisoners are made to live completely alone

**Spitfire** a British fighter plane used in World War II

**Stalag Luft III** a prisoner-of-war camp run by the German air force during World War II

# Index

## Web Finder

**Henri Charriere (Papillon)**
http://www.sinclairos.freeserve.co.uk/Papillon/PAPILLON1.htm
**Roger Bushell**
http://www.pbs.org/wgbh/nova/greatescape/three.html
**The Dalai Lama**
http://www.dalailama.com/
**Frank Morris and John and Clarence Anglin**
http://www.alcatrazhistory.com/
**Dith Pran**
http://www.dithpran.org/

*Answers from page 25:*
*claustrophobia=fear of narrow spaces; acrophobia=fear of heights; noctiphobia=fear of night; aquaphobia=fear of water; achluophobia=fear of darkness*